*"An evolving vision
met with continual action
will manifest its reality."*

Adam Cummins (Adzy C.)

Written by Adam Cummins (Adzy C.)
Edited by Adam Cummins (Adzy C.)
Illustrated By Réka Kárpát
www.DeveoStudio.com
Final Revisions By Adam Cummins (Adzy C.)

BLUES take a VACATION

by Adzy C.

illustrated by Réka Kárpát

In a world filled with color,
existed the hues and shades.
There were also the tints and also the tones;
all coloring and unafraid.

Blues decided to take a vacation.
They had colored more than most.
Coloring the sky was endless work,
as well as the oceans from coast to coast.

With the **Blues** gone, the white space
became vast.
Other colors decided to take on
the **Blues'** tasks.

The oceans were colored orange,
and the sky was made of jade!
Change was happening fast,
leaving many colors afraid.

Maroons marooned themselves;
scared of the orange sea.

Some **Yellows** went bananas,
when they saw the sky's new green.

Gray was shocked,
at the newly colored rocks.

Greens and Browns abandoned ground;
some Reds were running rampant.
Colors screamed, "the end is near!"
The changes for some were tragic.

Amidst it all, the Whites were laughing.
Whites were used to change.
They remembered a white world so boring,
before the colors came.

The Blues came back, ready to color,
and awed at the brand new scene.
Had Blues been too selfish?
Should they have shared the sky and sea?

A committee of colors came together,
with one of each to represent.
They pondered, suggested, and soon manifested,
solutions to try make sense.

Jade pleaded, "Please take back the sky.
Many Jades are tired,
and some are afraid of heights."

Then Blue said, "We can do it again.
Does anyone have an objection, my friends?"

Blacks suggested they make a dark night.
Blues could rest from making daylight.
White and Gray chimed in to say,
"A night could use a lesser light."

Yellow said, "I'll make the sun set and rise,
to let colors know if it's day or night time."
Red, Pink and Orange would help with the sun.
Together, a beautiful sight had begun.

But Oranges liked their new orange sea.
It made them seem important, you see?
Orange declared, "You can't have it back!
Why should oceans be blue, in fact?"

"It doesn't", said Blue. "But, please understand.
The coloring is vast from the depths to the sand.
Blues blend well from the abyss to the surface.
We have billions of Blues,
                    so we know we can do this."

Oranges said, "We didn't think of that.
We wouldn't have enough of us;
enough to stay on track."

All the colors soon agreed,
that the Blues should continue.
Oranges would have the time,
to keep oranges on the menu.

Then Green and Brown asked,
      "What about the Reds?
Surely, we don't want red ground instead?"
Red disagreed, "What do you mean?
Red looks better than Brown and Green."

On this note they tallied a vote;
Votes were carefully counted.
Greens and Browns would return to ground,
leaving the Red dumbfounded.

Green then told Red, "You are pretty, we know.
Do you think you could get
more red flowers to grow?"
Red said, "Of course! We're a color of passion.
We will make a flower only **love** can imagine!"

The colors kept meeting;
discussing things of change.
They voted with good intention;
all acknowledged as their base.

It wasn't always perfect,
and it wasn't always grand.
But, the colors tried real hard,
to think of all and the world at hand.